MOORESVILLE PUBLIC LIBRARY
220 W. HARRISON ST
MOORESVILLE, IN 46158
317-831-7323

FELIX CULPA

FELIX CULPA

a novel

JEREMY GAVRON

SCRIBE
Melbourne • London

Scribe Publications
18–20 Edward St, Brunswick, Victoria 3056, Australia
2 John St, Clerkenwell, London, WC1N 2ES, United Kingdom

Published by Scribe 2018

Copyright © Jeremy Gavron 2018

All rights reserved. Without limiting the rights under copyright reserved above,
no part of this publication may be reproduced, stored in or introduced into
a retrieval system, or transmitted, in any form or by any means (electronic,
mechanical, photocopying, recording or otherwise) without the prior written
permission of the publishers of this book.

The moral rights of the author have been asserted.

Typeset in Minion Pro

Printed and bound in the UK by CPI Group (UK) Ltd, Croydon CR0 4YY

Scribe Publications is committed to the sustainable use of natural resources
and the use of paper products made responsibly from those resources.

9781925322620 (Australian edition)
9781911344766 (UK edition)
9781925548426 (e-book)

CiP records for this title are available from the British Library
and the National Library of Australia.

This book is largely composed of phrases and sentences from one hundred
other books, carefully selected and arranged in order to deliver a cumulative
new meaning under the fair creative use rules.

scribepublications.com.au
scribepublications.co.uk

For Judy, Leah and Mima,

the oldest song of all,

and for Clare Alexander,

steadfast and true.

1

Never open a book with weather. Never use the word 'suddenly'. If it sounds like writing, rewrite it.

But what if a story begins with weather? What if a writer goes to work in a prison in a long gypsy summer and the world turns? Suddenly turns.

A modern prison. Redbrick buildings. Lawns, flower beds.

Even a pond in the middle, in which it is said there were once fish until they were caught and fried up on the wings.

A former military airfield — you can still see the shape of the runway cutting across the prison grounds and into the neighbouring cornfield like the ghost of some ancient ley line.

Writer in residence.

Though he does not reside here and does not appear to be much of a writer. He comes into the prison three days a week, wanders the wings, sits with the men in their cells, looking at their writing, but mostly listening to their talk.

Listener in residence, then.

Privy to the secret griefs of wild, unknown men.

The world turning all the while, really, though he is not aware of it, does not hear its creakings, the songs of the air.

Not that much of a listener, either.

Thinking his own thoughts while the prisoners tell their stories.

Taking a man outside to sit on a hump of grass and closing his eyes to the warm sun.

Gypsy summer, old wives' summer, all-hallown summer, little summer of the quince.

The sun shining bright before the storm blast.

And then there came both mist and snow and it grew wondrous cold.

Or at least mist and snow in the north of the country and rain in the south, where the prison is, where the city is where he lives.

Rain against my window.

Lying on the sofa of the kitchenette apartment he had rented on 17th Street.

The malodorous sofa.

A pile of half-read books beside him.

Though the worst of the weather is soon over and he drives in to the prison through the tail end of the storm.

The windswept grounds empty.

The windows on the wings closed against the cold.

Smells of sweat, sperm and blood.

Fug of tobacco.

Prisoners loitering on the spurs, the landings.

Three men were standing very close together, the middle one of them holding a folded-up newspaper which the other two were studying over his shoulder.

Seen this?

The paper thrust at him.

The prisoners growing used to him now, this writer fellow who walks among them in civvies, comes into their cells without deadlocking the doors, drinks the tea they offer without worrying they have put bleach in it, urinated in it.

Wrote letters for the men.

At least until the prison scribes took him aside to explain that he was undercutting the wing economy.

Looks down at the newspaper. Takes in a headline about a body found in the snow, the blurry mugshot of an adolescent boy.

That's Felix, isn't it.

He was in here until not so long ago.

A hiker, the newspaper calls him, caught out in the storms. In the hills in the north.

What was he doing up there?

Most of the residents of the prison young men from the city who had hardly been out of their neighbourhoods until they were sent away.

That's the question.

Not hiking, not dressed like that.

Probably drugs.

Nonces.

Lucre.

He nods, hands back the newspaper. He is growing used to the prisoners, too, their ways, their stories. This writer who does not write among these men who are here because they have lost the plot, lost the thread of their own lives.

2

There, beyond the bamboos, begins the path.

Though he does not see it.

Continues on around the wings, walks over to the stores to talk to a man about a poem, to the segregation unit to see a prisoner who sent a message that he has a tale to tell.

Set himself alight on his wife's doorstep and when she opened the door clasped her to him.

Lifts his shirt to show the scars.

To the workshops, too, perhaps, in the old airplane hangar, or the gardens, or the kitchens, to return a piece of writing with which he has been entrusted, read an appeal, hear a confession.

Until, at the day's end, the men banged up for the night, he collects his coat from the education office, hands in his keys at the gate, passes out through the set of doors they call the airlock.

Soft black asphalt road and the tall hibiscus.

String of scattered suburbs.

Back into the city.

A shambling second-floor back which overhung the railway and rocked to the passing trains.

Reflected headlights slowly slid the wall.

His days off he sleeps, leafs through books, the writings the prisoners give him.

The smell of the wings still on the paper.

Walks through the city.

Losing himself among unknown streets and hardly bothering in which direction he was going.

The manuscript he had been working on abandoned to the dust.

Other things, too.

For whom would he set himself alight?

Though it is not quite true that he is not writing.

In his pocket an old half-used notebook he has turned round and begun scrawling in from the back frontwards.

Spidery handwriting full of crossings-out and corrections.

Fragments, nonsense syllables, exclamations.

Observations which he found scribbled on the walls of subway washrooms.

Overhears in the streets.

In the cafe where he sometimes takes his meals.

Eavesdropping, if necessary, and writing down whatever I heard them say that sounded revealing to me.

Foraging in used bookstores.

Picking all sorts of details from the tomes that lay open in front of him.

Pieces, it seems to him, of other stories, yet to be told.

Hears in the prison, too.

The talk, for a day or two more, of the boy in the snow.

Smallish, frail figure.

Always had paint in his hair and on his hands.

Killed and dropped here.

The body, it turns out, found in a t-shirt and trousers, without socks or shoes.

Some way from the nearest road or trail.

Probably off his head in some country shebeen, went out to paint the snow yellow and got lost.

This one of the old lags. Old wisdom. Old humour, too.

Wanted a relief map, the joke went.

Is so life is.

Here in the shadow of the walls.

3

Use regional dialect, patois, sparingly. Avoid detailed descriptions of characters. Leave out the parts that readers tend to skip.

But which parts are these exactly? And which readers? And what if these are the parts that prevail on a writer?

The haze in the beerhall.

The mutterings of drunks and crazy people.

The old jailbird's song.

Tottered about the streets.

Collecting stories about the divided city.

Divided stories.

Might mean anything and nothing, allusive, blurred as the back of a piece of embroidery, a tangle of knots and threads.

11

Lingering on the wings beyond his hours.

Played dominoes with the prisoners in the evenings.

Gradually being drawn in.

What they had to say about their jobs, love affairs, vittles, sprees, scrapes.

The singularity of thievery.

Safe-breakers, cat-men.

Specialist who picked locks with his celluloid shirt collar.

The extraordinary calmness one feels at the moment of performing the theft.

Listens like a three years' child.

Inhaled the odours of stone, of urine, bitterly tonic, the smells of rust and of lubricants, felt the presence of a current of urgency.

The strength necessary for departing from conventional morality.

Occurred to me that, if I wished, I could, at that moment, run out into the street, and, with vulgar expletives of lust, embrace any woman I chose; or shoot the first person I met.

Return to them in their vicious prison as one of themselves.

Hand over my shoelaces, belt, wallet.

Penal code's all wrong.

Lists everything you mustn't do in life, stealing, murdering, receiving stolen goods, but it doesn't say a word about what you should do.

What remedy can there be.

Day melted into another.

Lived to himself in his little room.

Speaking only to order his food in the cafe where he sometimes takes his meals.

As one autumn cockcrow.

A kind of melancholy aspect about the morning that making him shiver.

Having neglected to bring a book or a prisoner's writings to read, he reaches for a newspaper left on the table and turning the pages comes to a report of the inquest of the boy in the snow.

13

The same blurry mugshot.

Twenty-two years of age. Last known address a hostel in the east of the city. In breach of his licence.

Died from exposure.

No trace of alcohol or drugs in his blood.

No injuries except for some scratches on his lower limbs.

Not uncommon in the advanced stages of hypothermia for the sufferer to remove his clothes.

Paradoxical undressing.

Muscles directing energy to the vital organs fail, blood surges to the extremities, fooling the brain into thinking the body is hot.

Expect to find his garments and footwear when the snow melts.

Held the paper up to better light.

Looking for clues in the camera's description.

Biographies in the line of a face.

Too young for the prison when it was taken, with all that suggests, but otherwise nothing to remark on.

Could look at him then look away and not remember what you'd seen.

Puts down the paper, turns back to his food.

Is not as if this fellar is his brother or cousin or even friend; he don't know the man from Adam.

But we cannot choose what reaches us from the face of a
newspaper, the gram of a plasticate...

Fishermen fishing from below...

Young taikid shrouded in mystery

Died in this strange place

Nothing made it my business...

Walks to his local library to be...

Shepherd came on the corpse

Bare rugged country

No sign of any other human...

Accounts of the affair came as close to the truth as newspaper
stories usually come.

4

But we cannot choose what speaks to us from the page of a newspaper, the grain of a photograph.

Fishermen fishing from bridges, the painters who paint them.

Young jailkid shrouded in mystery.

Died in this strange place.

Nothing made it my business except curiosity.

Walks to his local library to look up the original news reports.

Shepherd came on the corpse.

Bare, rugged country.

No sign of any other human presence.

Accounts of the affair came as close to the truth as newspaper stories usually come.

Stowaway spilled from the undercarriage of a descending airplane.

Victim of a big cat farmers claim has been taking sheep.

Beast escaped from a travelling circus.

Wash pants torn.

Excluded the impossible, whatever remains, however improbable, must be the truth.

Though a different truth once the boy was named.

A killer himself, it turns out.

Terrible case of an old woman who lived by herself and because she resisted some young men who broke in they took her life.

Regular gang of young ruffians.

Ladronés muy famosos.

Though the boy the only one apprehended or even identified.

Ain't a fizgig.

Won't shop no one.

Won't reveal anything else now.

Took his dreadful secrets to the grave.

Though it occurs to our writer that he has access to information the newspapers did not.

Asks for permission to consult the prison archives.

File I'd like to peruse.

Tomb world.

Shelving installed from ceiling to floor.

Runs his fingers over the dusty folders.

How many bewildering secrets are contained within.

Raw materials for the characterisation.

Finding the boy's, he carries it to the table, unties the string, spreads out the papers.

Reports, applications, memorandums, sheets, files, copies of pages from wing occurrence books.

On this day the prisoner was admitted.

Transferred.

Employed in the laundry.

Found bleeding after a commotion on the 2s landing on C wing.

Starts at the beginning with his pre-sentence report.

Accounts of his early relations with police.

Broke into a newsagent with two other juveniles and stole confectionary and cigarettes.

Age of eleven or twelve.

Living with his mother.

Never was too smart at formal schooling.

A day-dreamer, his teachers wrote on report cards — standoffish and shy and withdrawn.

Further arrests at fourteen and fifteen for trespass, breaking and entering.

Loose notions concerning the rights of property.

Seventeen when, with accomplices unknown, he committed

the offences for which he was sent away.

Broke in at the pantry window.

Commission of the burglary when the victim walked in through her front door.

Took a couple of crazy steps and fell full length and lay still.

Trial by a jury of his peers.

Never see such an out-and-out young wagabond, your worship.

Preached a long sermon at him.

Goes to a house with the intention to break in and steal.

Embarks upon a crime he is morally guilty of any other crime which may spring from it.

Law says you be old enough.

Take him away.

Began a passage through many hands.

Straight to reform school.

Empty your pockets.

Blanket and a pannikin and spoon.

Night in the dorm.

Suppose yer the new boy, ain't yer?

Blood flowing from nose and mouth and ears.

Sooner take a blow than give one.

Spell in the seg.

Like the room of a Russian saint.

Hours to commune with his own thoughts.

Learned your place.

Good dog and all'll go well and the goose hang high.

Transferred eventually to the adult system.

Spent his days uneventfully going along with prison routine.

Admitted into the paint crew.

Certificate of competence in the use of a brush, kettle, cutting in, sugar soaping.

Cell of his own.

Notice of illness of member of immediate family.

Eres huerfano.

Chaplaincy memorandum.

Good chat with him and gave him a copy of the good book.

Let not the lad go astray in the darkness.

Licence granted after four years and three months.

Signed for his clothes, his discharge grant.

Goodly sum of personal cash.

Passed through several strong gates.

Entered into what had been wall to him and bathed in the substance that composed it.

5

Much that is in the files is cryptic.

Told a special kind of truth. They didn't lie, but they were formal.

Left out a lot of important things — often essential things — that local people would know and gossip about.

Though when he asks around the prison, the boy seems to have left little impression.

Don't talk much.

Hollowness and neglect of somebody of no account.

Meagreness of his body merely emphasised by the blue overalls.

In jail a man has no personality. He is a minor disposal problem and a few entries on reports. Nobody cares who loves him or hates him, what he looks like, what he did with his life.

Nobody reacts to him unless he gives trouble.

This his personal officer.

Personal opinion is that he wasn't all there.

Wouldn't apply for leave to attend his own mother's funeral.

Grant him special parole but he stubbornly refused.

Though a good worker, according to the painting instructor.

Does be polite and say thank you.

Painting with his crew over the graffiti that will bloom again on the same walls tomorrow or the next day.

Quiet just because he ain't have anything to say.

Ain't no law about talkin' or smilin'.

Though an old lag he consults gives him another perspective.

Didn't know the boy, but knows the wings.

Plenty in here not right in the head.

Hideous howlings and yellings.

Confounded zoo.

But playing the fool can also be a method of survival. No one's going to ask an idiot to deliver product or hide a tool in his cell.

Commandments of prison life.

Speak little and if questioned reply as briefly as possible.

Take up as little space.

Living very sparing on our provisions.

What you don't order from the commissary can't be taken from you.

Explains why the boy had cash to carry out.

Surplus earnings.

Religion a solace for some, but a bible has other uses. Roll-up paper, other kinds of paper.

Cleanliness next to godliness.

Though body odour has its benefits.

Feculence a barrier.

Prison its own belief system.

Method of accepting things without questioning the why and the wherefore.

The variable airs, the large and small events.

The only problem that after a while you can forget what it is like to be normal.

Men who are nothing allow themselves to become nothing.

What's needed here, my friend, is discretion, a good nose, presence of mind, steady nerves.

Yes, indeedy.

6

In the street little eddies of wind were whirling dust and torn paper into spirals.

Chin nuzzled into his breast.

Prison was no more than a small walled village.

What does Caborca know of Huisiachepic?

Rise now and go about the city.

Fugitive's trail.

In the streets and in the broad ways.

Eastern suburbs of the town.

Emerged at last into a small road lined with old gloomy houses.

Through a wooden gate.

Hammers on the brown door.

Hostel noted in the boy's file, referred to in the newspapers as his last address.

Shabby genteel place.

On the walls were faded frescoes and faded traces of a painted dado.

Corridor smelt of formalin.

Figure of a woman blocked out the light from the office.

Warden of the hostel.

Can I help you?

Dimly remember him. Wasn't there some sort of trouble?

Newspapers took up this curious case.

Not one of ours.

Hadn't been in there, hadn't passed by.

Might have been on the waiting list. Always have more applicants than we have beds.

Talk to his probation officer.

Lo siento.

Drizzle of rain.

Walked toward the phone booth.

Dialled the number.

Voice spoke through the lisp of the rain.

Seeing as he's no longer with us I suppose it's alright to talk.

Dead dog never bit nobody.

Put him in temporary accommodation until a place freed up at the hostel.

Residing at the time in furnished lodgings.

Only he didn't reside very long.

Split for parts unknown.

What the hell you expect?

A dozen policemen disguised as sheikhs, cowboys and Spaniards on his tail?

Take down particulars but case like that so common.

Fifty like him on my books.

Poor little slum-bred hard guys that got knocked over on their first caper.

Authorities would have their work cut out if they were going to chase after every runaway.

Address she gives him is not far away and he sets out again.

Squat little streets.

Three small boys hunching knee to knee play cards beneath a black umbrella.

In a yard a plastic deer.

The lodgings, when he reaches them, spread across two houses.

Yellow vapour lights glowed high up in the air and a neon sign between them said, Welcome to Realito.

Number one cheap cheap hotel.

Watches the lights blinking.

Hell does he think he's doing.

Monster crouched in the shadows.

Only knew that at the bottom of each breath there was a hollow place that needed to be filled.

Something in the story itself to tell him about the way the world was.

Pass through the door.

A desk was back in the dimness and behind the desk a bald-headed man.

Raises an eyelid.

Takes a key off the hook.

Staircase into the bowels of the building.

Hall unlit like a subterranean cave.

Room wasn't much larger than a broom closet.

Bed, a chair, a coloured print of Killarney, and a barred window looking out on a wall.

What's your grift then?

Think I can't smell a dick when I meet one.

Where a man's at ain't necessarily for you to know.

Got my wallet unstuck from the lower part of my back and spread tired-looking dollar bills along the bed.

Stared at me for a long level minute.

Thin arse little man.

Week maybe two.

Gay Paree.

How should I know?

Fuckin' AWOL.

Do know is that he left without signing his chits.

Care so much about him maybe you'd care to settle his debts?

Leaned forward and brought his face up close to mine.

Ever get socked in the kisser?

Nose into our business and you'll wake up in an alley with the cats looking at you.

Beat it before I change my mind.

7

Slunk down the street.

Rain beatin' on him and he don't even know it.

Like one of those small men in gangster films who know too much and get killed.

Good that god kept the truths of life from the young as they were starting out or else they'd have no heart to start at all.

Perhaps that's all that happened — the boy lost heart.

Went to jail part of me had died.

Hills finished the job.

Knows too much and knows nothing.

Last name in his notebook.

Youth worker who signed the pre-sentence report.

Ring fifteen times.

Said he was in court and would not be available until late in the afternoon.

Walks the streets until the appointed hour.

Called at the offices.

Wait if he's busy.

Walls have plenty notice hang up.

Carrying a knife isn't sharp. Real men use protection. Get ahead not arrested.

Slick-haired blonde man opened the door.

Good god! he said. Haven't you got anything better to do with your time?

Spare you a few minutes as you are here.

Voice was already down the hall.

Eastern tales of woe.

Comes from the squalor of their streets, the filth of their homes.

Murderers and robbers from their very cradle.

Though something different about the boy, he admits, when they are seated in his office.

Lives in a world all his own.

Monkey, you know.

Smaller one used by bigger ones to access properties.

Thing Felix could do.

Break and enter a window without smashing glass.

Convenient drainpipe.

Tickle the lock.

Supple pull-up Felix gets in.

Softly up the steps straight afore you and along the little hall to the street door, unfasten it and let us in.

Why he was the one put away.

Fingered by his prints on the window, the inside of the front door.

Not because he was the instigator.

Captain or corrovat.

Arrest were banal.

In lieu of the dogged black-visaged ruffian they had expected to behold there lay a mere child.

What were his motives, or did he have motives?

Attempts of the police and the public prosecutor's office to find this out have been fruitless.

Never saw him with money or possessions.

Sharp clothes.

Brain worked in dim ways.

Claimed he didn't know the old woman was hurt, that he went back out the window when she appeared.

Door closed behind the others as they fled.

Nobody don't know nothing until the milk bottles start to pile up.

Broke her hip in the fall but it was dehydration that killed her.

Explained that to him, he said if he'd have known he would have gone back and given her a drink of water.

Odd thing to say.

Long sentence for a juvenile but a life was lost.

Refused to give any names.

Judges don't like that, though it's the law round here.

Anybody that belonged to the band told the secrets he must have his throat cut and then have his carcass burnt up.

Bonds that come with blood.

Never been able to discover who is his father.

Notwithstanding the most superlative, and I may say supernat'ral, exertions on the part of this parish.

As for the north I have wondered myself what took him up there.

Run a scheme sending kids kayaking, abseiling, orienteering.

Hills in the south.

Never went but perhaps he heard about it from someone who

39

did. After his time away thought he'd have himself a holiday.

Prison is where you promise yourself the right to live.

Fulfil the dreams of one's youth.

Only he bought a ticket to the wrong hills.

8

Still going into the prison, reading the men's writings, listening to their talk.

Fascinating facts and tales from the poky.

Pale wall of dreams.

Standing in a cell one evening while its occupant brews tea in the wing kitchen.

Hung with old calendars and magazine pictures.

High narrow slit of a window.

Looked out on a bare courtyard lit by electric lamps.

Full of the melancholy which seeps into the bones in prison at night.

Always get into those places. What is hard is to get out.

Hole in the wall, a gap in the barbed wire.

The black-bordered finger-thick dividing line.

Except that the dividing line doesn't always run along the concrete balustrade.

Two or three days and nights went by.

Cold grey day.

Headed for the projects.

Poke 'em where they live a little bit 'n' see what happens.

Or at least where the boy used to live with his mother, according to his file.

Den in the farthest east of the city.

Said that premises retain some stamp, however faint, of their previous inhabitants.

Weather closing in as he arrives at the estate.

Milky fog.

Buildings looming like giant ghosts.

Woman points him the way.

No use trying the lift. Even at the best of times it was seldom working.

Ungarnished staircase.

Hallway smelt of boiled cabbage and old rag mats.

Dim-lit doorway.

Long time since he has stood at the threshold of any residence other than his own.

Bell which was so worn it rang only intermittently.

Door opened a crack. A woman's face.

Who might you be?

Wrong place, I expect.

Peered through the chink.

Not place, time.

What did he imagine?

Tuberstirrings in the blacksweet duff.

The boy's shape in the shadows.

This is where I used to sleep. My cot was against this wall.

This is where we used to have Christmas.

Though as the door closes he sees a movement in the window of the neighbouring apartment.

Curtain was drawn aside and a narrow intent face was close to the glass.

Snow-white hair.

Rang the bell, the door snapped open.

What you want young man?

Better come in.

Front room that had cotton lace antimacassars pinned on everything you could stick a pin into.

Can't be too careful these days.

Have a seat over on the couch.

People really bad mind, you know.

Came here twenty-two years ago we didn't lock our doors hardly.

Here when she brought the boy home from the hospital.

Little fellow in a bag.

Throat vibrating with a queer rasping noise.

When they took him away.
Local rozzers.

Fourteen hundred hours at the maternal domicile.

When they took her, too.

St John ambulance.

From that appointment she never came back.

Wasn't exactly the sort you get to know.

Don't have no visitors.

Floor dirty with footprint and cigarette butt.

Opinion is she drinks liquor.

As for his soul.

Ain't sure I could put a name to it.

Hours standing at the window.

Gazing from the smoky room inside the glass.

Seemed to wait for something.

Whatever it was didn't come, or turned out wrong.

Went and joined a set of thieves and bad characters and almost broke his mother's heart.

Shook her head.

Stands himself and walks to the window.

Lawn of weedy grass.

In a few high windows of the apartment towers violet and reddish lights gleam.

Far off the banshee wail of police or fire sirens.

Worked in the launderette the other side of those blocks.

Take him with her when he was small and lay him in one of them plastic baskets they used for the washing.

9

Wanders the estate, past the launderette which is boarded up now.

Between a slop shop and a gin shop.

Through the nearby streets.

Veil of lightly falling snow.

Little two-storey houses with battered doorways.

Walls cracking like the last days of Pompeii.

One of these perhaps where the old woman lay dying on the floor.

Little window that he got in at.

What went on inside those buildings.

Divide up in little worlds and you stay in the world you belong to and you don't know anything about what happening in the other ones except what you read in the newspapers.

Man beating their wife.

Lofts where families hide children.

Caresses of a murderer.

Police are pursuing their inquiries.

Complete story in tomorrow's weekend edition.

Stops to write in his notebook.

Faces glaring in suspicion, steam rising from beneath the street in frozen wisps.

Pen pressing into the paper.

Not so easy to find a man.

Get to the true facts.

The inside details that the newspapers never mention.

What his feelings were whom I pursued.

Why he behaved as he did.

Nobody, my mother said, knows anything about anyone else. Not even about a close neighbour. Not even about the person you are married to. Or about your parent or your child.

Even about ourselves we know nothing.

Each still lives behind the wall.

Wall in our heads.

Fog closes in and blurs the edges of the moment.

Tell me the story in your heart.

Er läßt sich nicht lesen.

You catch the snowflake but when you look in your hand you don't have it no more.

10

Well three or four months run along and it was well into the
winter now.

Still living in one room in this break-down old house.

Like a cave with the ancient black stove, the iron sink, the
green cupboards, the gas ring.

The divan where he frequently spent whole days reclining.

A whole day writing a single word.

Feelings, heart, everything in strange condition.

Beginning to take on the air of an ascetic and to neglect his
appearance.

Wasn't just that he grew a beard or stopped shaving regularly;
he didn't seem to care if the sole of his shoe came loose.

Heels tapped across the wilderness of the city.

Would sit for hours on the steps of abandoned buildings or next to puddles.

Dreamed I was far down in the depths.

At midnight he would wander through the roistering singers.

Looked keenly at everything, but he felt half blind.

The spark of life within flickered and went down. It was nearly out. He felt strangely numb.

Stood in front of the mirror, absently feeling the week-old stubble on his face.

The frailty of everything revealed at last.

A state of dulled inertia from which he tried helplessly to rouse himself.

Retreated into his private world, going through his old notebooks.

Maybe the story I'm looking for doesn't exist.

Poke my forefinger through him and would find nothing inside.

Only he could stop thinking, completely negate his own will power, he, too, might be sucked towards that place.

Finish with this arseness, you hear.

One grim winter evening when it had a kind of unrealness.

Fog sleeping restlessly over the city and the lights showing in the blur.

Roaming the powdered streets.

Reached that point of exhaustion and sleeplessness which produces a series of incandescent fantasies.

Sees someone in a square living a life or an instant that could be his.

Face was youthful but the perceptive observer could distinguish in it the traces of sorrow and experience.

Strict and literal truthfulness was a trivial game.

Always be stoppages, blockages, siltings, unsuccessful attempts at conduction.

You can write something and every sentence in it will be a fact, you can pile up facts, but it won't be true.

Search out the place where fact ended and imagination took over.

Door into a world of dreams.

Don't you see — he was simply the one who was to come.

Will serve me as a pilot.

Rose, unsteady, long, pale, indistinct, like a vapour exhaled by the earth, and swayed slightly, misty and silent.

Simply do what we always do in such cases: we tie a rope to the dog and let it walk and it will lead you.

11

Sunday in the eastern districts.

Feet had brought him back here of their own accord.

Moving through crowds.

Standing in doorways.

Scans the streets.

Face I see.

Touched him on the shoulder.

Pulled a dirty and wrinkled newspaper from the inside pocket of his greatcoat.

Did you ever know a young man?

Eyes lock for a second then dart away.

Talked to thin air.

Like someone throwing gravel at a street lamp.

Pen scratching at the silence.

Slumped in a doorway.

Slanting grey rain like a swung curtain.

Imagined the boy crouching down like a wild animal in the darkness.

Saw a small dark figure.

Brought the crouching shape up front in my mind.

Slipped out after him and followed him down the street.

Hood that overshadowed his face.

Lost in his clothes.

Stops in the shelter of a stairwell to light a cigarette.

Eyes blinked behind the swirling smoke.

Approached and stood still.

Sign of peace.

You've been following me around.

Don't guess I know you.

Looking for somebody.

Thought maybe you'd been seein' him.

Show him the photo.

Nuthin' t'say, officer.

Nothing to do with the police.

Huntin' my chap that's about all.

Considered that with some care.

Took the photograph.

Ain't seen him for quite a spell now.

Not since in the spring.

Sizeable world to set out huntin' somebody in.

Not exactly hunting.

Bones lay in the cemetery.

Searching for traces.

Eyes almost disappeared between the suddenly narrowed lids.

Lips went back against his teeth.

Don't know nuthin' about the dead.

Living when he passed by.

Not here for trouble.

Maybe you'd still know a thing or two.

What he was doing.

Thought about it, breathing slowly.

Can tell where he stayed.

Place his ma worked.

Where he worked.

He worked in the launderette?

Threw his cigarette on the cement floor.

Beckoning gesture.

Clanging stairs to the empty roof.

Rain had stopped.

City was a sea of lights.

See the place.

Four aluminium towers rise.

Skyscrapers with thousands of windows.

Cranes like straws.

Never did give me the straight of it but he liked it up there.

Painting those walls.

Did he say why he left? Did he mention any plans?

Dying ain't in people's plans, is it?

Maybe he met him a gal and went off.

Maybe have some other unknown future.

Further than that I do not know.

12

Does go to the laundry.

Fast closed and mouldering away.

Walks round the back.

Cobbled, stepped alleyway with its gutter in the middle for the mules' urine.

Rubbish bins with cheese rinds, greasy paper.

Little lattice window about five feet and a half above the ground.

Climbed to the barky lip.

Slipped my hand in and twisted the knob.

Crawled within.

Feet creaked and crackled over the bare planking.

Machines like the relics of some antique rite.

Old works of stone.

Wall from which the paper was hanging in ribbons.

Mould feeding on the plaster.

Small room at the back where someone appears to have been sleeping at some time past.

Bed of flattened cartons.

Gently recessed.

Knelt and placed his hand.

Dust has settled.

Droppings and mute prints.

In a corner some chewed wrappings and a tattered copy of a bible.

A leetle pocket-size one.

Also chewed into by some creature in search of nourishment.

Shape of its body in the layers.

Takes the book and his next day in the prison shows it to the chaplain.

Could be the one he gave the boy, but can't be sure.

O lord how manifold are thy works.

Seeks out also the painting instructor.

One who could know an answer.

Didn't deny it.

Telephoned this man about a job.

Good reliable worker he'd be prepared to take him on.

Off the books, of course.

Think it's easy to find legitimate employment?

Recent prison release order in my pocket.

Sorry the vacancy get filled.

Not asking for the sun or the moon.

Only want to get by.

Little food, a little place to sleep.

Writes down the number and in the evening he calls.

Looking for an employee of yours.

Former employee.

Don't talk to me about that boy.

Regular fool of a youth.

Had to let him go.

Slept on the premises.

Hide in the clothes closet.

Could have cost me the contract.

People in this world don't know how other people does affect their lives.

Hung the phone in my ear.

Morning he was standing by the side of the road at daybreak with a clean shirt and a pair of socks.

Brown woollen suit.

Homme marche dans la ville.

Cluster of tall buildings.

Interminably and hungrily going up.

Show apartment on the thirty-sixth floor.

Punched the roof button and the elevator silently rose.

Door came open on a small red-headed man who wore a tan suit.

Mouth snaked up as he chuckled.

Sky village.

New mode of life.

Radically new environment with its own internal landscape and logic, where old categories of thought would merely be an encumbrance.

Floor was covered with green and grey linoleum.

Contemporary furniture in the G-plan.

Arching above him the ceiling and upper walls.

Could be reconstructed to fit the expectations and particularities.

Contents arranged for the eye.

Look around a little.

Wondering as he does so what had drawn the boy to this place.

Opulence of human fantasy.

Comes to the edge.

Vast plate-glass window.

In front of him a tower still in construction.

Gleaming skeleton of a building going up, from which came the busy beat of hammers.

Beams hung from the cranes.

Dizzy drop into empty air.

Below the city laid out like a puzzle.

Wilderness of bricks and mortar.

Streets like the floors of valleys or dry river beds.

Rough and rudimentary like an artist's initial pencil sketches.

Something stirs in his heart.

A greatness and a vastness.

The way a bird must feel, free and loose.

One fine morning you find that the sky is light blue and there is nothing to weigh you down.

13

Own journeying began to take upon itself the shape of a tale.

Like a vagabond from place to place.

South, then east, then north.

Through the vastness.

The streets according to the pull and the feeling.

Labyrinth of dark narrow courts.

Little step-down taverns panelled with rum-soaked timbers.

Can I help you?

Just waiting for someone, I said to the bartender.

Ferreting around in every weird underworld he could find.

Winding alleys.

Dead ends.

Residence of none but low ruffians.

What you doin' sneakin' at the door?

Who are you looking for?

Guy who's spent five years in jail.

Diminutive in stature.

Unsociable and solitary like the true leopard.

Mother being a washerwoman.

In the evening, when I was at home, I wrote it all down in a notebook.

Till two or three o'clock in the morning.

Piled desk.

Head outlined by a halo of light.

Climbing the gulley between the mountains of books.

Take down another and again turn the pages.

Make a note in pencil in the margin.

Look long and earnestly at the curious figures.

Secret messages in literature.

Writing in a small notebook.

No doubt that those jottings contained a description.

Each one in its proper place in the puzzle.

Could only find the right path.

Two, three weeks go by.

Damp streets after the rain.

Feet slithered on the sidewalks.

Neighbourhood at the edge.

Came to a hall in ruins.

A place where hobos had drawn up crates to sit over fires.

Pipes black with soot.

Stout old gentleman, rather lame in one leg.

Features cracked and crazed.

Sit on this blanket. Have a smoke.

Lifted a wrinkled paw.

Gestured toward the fire.

Lost peoples that were never talked about in the newspapers.

Unable to separate their own identities from the cities where they had spent their lives.

Condemned to wander forever in an inner desert.

Gaze had become steady.

Pose of a buddha.

Not all those who wander are lost.

Ways of living in that vast city.

Outside the normal world of time and place.

Beyond a line of his own making.

Obey his own law.

Glimpse one's own true nature.

See the world the wolf saw.

This is the heart of the matter, everything else is only a shadow.

Esto es la verdad.

14

Not what you look at but what you see.

Go over things again.

More to the root of things.

Library's basements where the incunabula were kept.

Old newspapers.

Something he had missed.

Number to contact with information about the boy.

People who knew him or were acquainted with him.

Dialled the operator and when she came on the line I asked her for long distance.

Voice at the other end of the telephone line sounded like wind.

Cool hardness of a cop.

Don't think anything.

Investigation has been called off.

Which the crime had been committed?

Wasn't used to this part of the world.

Not thought of such cold weather and was surprised to see it come.

Meteorology is not superfluous to the story.

Geographical features.

Where he was found is desolate even on a good day.

Grass and bracken and you may hear the forlorn crying of the titihoya.

Accidents in life and he met with a bad one.

Theories to the contrary are the merest moonshine.

Voice grew icicles.

Like I told you case is closed.

Didn't find his clothes because we didn't look for them.

Don't get the idea all police are stupid. Some could take the shoes off the likes of you and you'd be walking barefoot.

Why anyone goes to the hills.

Escape from the commonplaces of existence.

Stayed with someone he met inside, perhaps.

Scoundrels of the north.

Village borders where the lepers and the lunatics, the horse thieves and the prostitutes live.

Our little country crimes.

Logged a few calls if I remember rightly.

File stored among countless others at the prefecture of police.

Send you the transcripts if I can dig them up.

No pleasure out of a corpse.

Just don't say where you got them from.

Hush, hush, confidential.

Keep your nose clean and everything will be jake.

15

Policeman's words lay inside me.

Detective instinct to tie everything that happens into one compact knot.

What's in the books.

Point very straight to one thing.

But if you shift your own point of view a little.

Story of something more — exactly what I couldn't tell.

Depends on the glass we see through.

Events narrated in the last chapter were yet but two days old.

Letter, umfundisi.

Creased manila envelope.

Opened it slowly and carefully.

20 ruled pages (9" x 12" approx) roughly torn along left-hand margin.

Collected extant data.

Name, an address, a neighbourhood, a background.

Yes I knew this young man.

Know him from the photograph.

Remember the first time I saw him.

Standing by a lamp post.

Walking up a cobbled street.

One night in the alleys of the old town.

The second-hand bookstore district.

Village churchyard sitting on a mossy gravestone.

Narrow little creek the blades of sunlight falling through the foliage.

Stumbling down into the rainy dark.

The lone clay trail.

North across the flat bleak landscape.

Westward into the jungle.

The Arab trading routes to the interior.

Boy with sleepy eyes.

Eyes were endlessly searching.

Like a dog.

A strange lank bird.

Old cap that was brown one time.

Bunch of grass in his hand.

Said he had a beautiful singing voice which spellbound all the senoritas.

Said he kept notches on his gun.

Said all sorts of things.

Way he walked on the outsides of his feet.

Love for his mother.

How the kid escaped.

Warn't ever murdered at all.

Became a jockey in Colombia.

Was with the Guatemalan guerrilla fighters.

A mythic figure.

A rumour in the city.

See only in the middle distance, in the hazes of heat, moving on his little green chariot, or wandering on foot.

Small toiling figure, head down and determined.

Ring a ding dillo.

Thousands of truths in the world.

Million decisions.

Who will live or die, who will fall in love or be unfaithful, who will make a fortune or make a fool of himself.

Writer's craft to pull from the myriad possibilities of all that could happen those that did and had to happen.

16

Day in early March when the weather had already warmed.

Walked up Chadbourne Street to the Eagle Cafe.

Meet a doctor from the transcripts.

Surgeon in the neighbourhood, known through a circuit of ten miles around.

Don't believe he still practiced.

Velveteen coat.

Locks of dry white hair clung to his scalp.

Ah so it is thou. Sit down.

Corner table was always reserved.

Walk over every day.

Was thinking about Felix.

The private and the public grotesque.

Nothing brightened up a front page so much as a story about human suffering.

Wanted to put things straight kind of.

Memory of him had remained dormant, but now it has suddenly come flooding back.

Circumstances attending his birth.

Naming responsibility.

Didn't deliver the child himself.

Layin' on o' hands is my best holt — for cancer, and paralysis, and sich things.

Wasn't even born in the hospital.

Floor of his mother's workplace.

Still attached to her when they arrived on the ward.

Pearly cord going from her stomach.

Baby only come by accident, you hear.

So she claimed.

Old story, he said, shaking his head. No wedding ring.

Got a father but you can't never find him.

Result of a few nights' rapport early in the year.

No point in pressing questions for the woman might not know herself.

Waters spilled from her she thought it was one of the washers.

Duty fell to a customer.

Ease a baby boy from her bloodied loins.

Take upon himself the office of respiration.

Blew on it until finally the child moved and began to cry.

Heard the story went to see.

Babies is something I never can believe.

Littlest chap.

Cowled in his blanket.

Eyes had not been open long yet already he could see with steady clearness.

Must have muttered aloud the phrase that came into his mind.

Mother heard his words.

Recognised one for a name and gave it to the boy.

O happy desart.

Little rag of life two days old come into this world of sins.

Don't know why I am telling you all this. I guess when a man has nothing better to do than to spit blood and try to hang on to his life he talks more than is good.

Hounded by a kind of remorse or shame.

Should have cared for him better.

Provide a child with a name you have a duty to him.

Never met one outlaw, including the kid, who had studied to be one.

Surgeon mournfully shaking his head.

Seemed especially troubled by the fact of the robbery.

A house broken into, said the doctor.

The old lady home.

Such is our story — it comes from darkness, wanders around, and returns to darkness.

Mors certa, vita incerta.

17

Another entry in the transcripts.

Took pity on him because he had no place to go.

Address poste restante.

Wrote a letter and received one in turn.

Suggested a meeting place.

Corner of Rue Saint Jacques.

Thought it was a boy with very short hair.

Red and black check shirt, dungaree trousers and heavy boots badly worn.

What's your interest in the kid?

Hair he saw refused to go with the voice he heard.

Girl's small figure.

He knew you or sumpin'?

Gaze was so sharp he couldn't speak for a moment.

Not so much that this man and I are friends. Rather there is a thread between us.

Looked at him with such obvious suspicion.

How do I know who you are?

What sort of man you are?

One who's been running all over the city.

Tryin' to catch him up.

Body straightened and with her hand she smoothed her dark hair.

So you're a writer.

I'm not anything.

Only tell you once — she touched her nose slightly — this nose can smell a lie.

Suddenly all the fountains of the great deep were opened.

Lost all the languages he had spoken.

Fluent stream of words awakens suspicion within me.

Prefer stuttering for in stuttering I hear the friction and the disquiet.

Theft whose poem I am writing.

Trying to build something out of old stones.

Hoped by expressing them in a form that they themselves imposed to construct an order.

Told her everything.

And the boy?

Seemed somehow to throw a kind of light on everything about me — and into my thoughts.

Stood there awhile saying nothing.

Glad if these pages rescued him from oblivion, though that oblivion is his own doing.

What you wanna know?

How did you meet him?

Knit her eyebrows.

All this running you probably haven't eaten a thing.

Go on a little trip, I'll explain on the way.

Motioned to me to follow her.

Traffic jams at the crossroads and hurrying crowds.

Shop windows and cafes light up.

Turned down a narrow street.

Nothing for us amongst all those cars and stores.

Ceased believing in the existence of that life.

Under the railway bridge.

Believed that in the world was another agenda.

Unfettered by any sort of traditions.

Ducked through a hole in the fence.

Back of a supermarket.

94

Sour reek of the refuse carts.

Lifted the lids one by one.

Dustbins to overflowing with quite eatable food.

Source of a successful squatter's wealth.

Poverty frees them from ordinary standards of behaviour.

Bread and vegetables were pitched away.

Baker's bread — what the quality eat — none of your low-down corn pone.

Strawberries and such truck.

Baloney and cheese.

Though she does not take the baloney.

Eat only vegetarian food.

Found Felix on the street one night.

Grab a loaf and run, swallowing it before they catch you.

Showed him all that could be freely obtained.

Aren't just a thief.

Didn't hoard food or deal on the black market.

Food was thrown away from deliberate policy, rather than that it should be given to the tramps.

Insulting you in huge wasteful piles.

Took the boy home for a meal cooked from the evening's forage.

He should do the same.

Come back with her and share the spoils.

Wrong to write about people without living through at least a little of what they are living through.

18

Started walking again and I followed along.

Seemed to find it natural that I should remain at her side.

Handing out food to beggars along the way.

Help the weak even if it means sharing our last crust of bread.

Societies to which I have been exposed seemed to me largely machines for the suppression of women.

The poor, the dispossessed.

Kind of fool to them.

Foreigners in our own country.

Everywhere we go we are told to go somewhere else.

Lookin' for a new way.

Without church or government or army, where each man alone would be his private government.

World which is the reverse of the customary world.

Twists of street and alley.

Ravine of tall leprous houses lurching towards one another.

Dark and shuttered like sunken wrecks.

Down some stone steps.

Rough boards which supplied the place of door and window were wrenched from their positions to afford an aperture wide enough for the passage of a human body.

Kind of cellar.

Up a rickety unlighted staircase.

Illumination coming dully from shuttered windows two and three storeys up.

Coconut oil lamp.

Old couch.

On it a girl was lying dressed in a frock of red velvet.

Young man with hair growing low on his head.

Pale sticky child.

You thought no one lived in this building. You thought it was abandoned.

Squatters had taken over.

Blankets and potato sacks have been spread over the bare floorboards.

Against the wall is an upended orange box.

Sit here while she prepares the food.

Tiled stove in the corner.

Smell of kerosene and frying oil.

Child sat carving a potato into the shape of a doll.

Young man rises and speaks.

On the theory of anarchy, on the necessity for political and personal freedom, and on his contempt for the moral law.

Scavengers were proud people and stood for no nonsense from anybody.

Reseats himself.

Eat from plates on their laps.

Excellent dinner from the leavings.

Afterwards she shows him around the building.

Ascending the darkened stairs.

Corner the boy made his own for the days he stayed.

Slept there curled up like a cat.

Not read the newspapers.

Chance she saw his photograph on a page she used to wrap food she was gathering.

Had to look three times before I was certain that it was indeed he.

Met him could hardly make out his features.

Coated with a thick layer of grime.

Slept in doorways.

Under culverts, behind hedges, in alleys.

Running away from something and it figured to be the law.

Not her custom to ask her guests for their identification papers or a police certificate of good conduct.

Offended no one and spoke little.

Never heard him refer to his relations and hardly ever to his own early life.

Evident that he wanted to cut things short in everything concerning himself.

One day he simply took off.

Ain't held here.

Essentially I think he is a solitary.

Something had happened to him that made him want to be by himself.

In every family there is one who is different and the others believe that they know that person but they do not.

Sees things that others do not see.

Flowers that shrank in the dusk and came forth again at the moon's rising.

Versions of time past and visions of time to come.

No names for the things she saw.

Certain that there are human qualities still to be discovered.

Natural laws of our own time were also temporary laws that would soon be replaced by new ones.

Inside me there are no frontiers or customs and I can travel as far as the farthest stars.

Come now to the top of the house.

Room was an attic.

Pipes and electrical wires hung down from the ceiling, but the bed by the window was made, the blankets on it folded carefully.

Shelf supported by red bricks.

On top a few colourful stones and a thick red candle.

Reached out suddenly and touched me.

Clothes smelled of forage.

Tiny thin arms.

You can have a poke, she said. If you want one.

Wouldn't charge you.

Naw, he said. I don't want nothin'.

You excuse me.

19

Lo the winter is past.

Mild and dewy morning.

Follows another lead from the transcripts down to the canal.

Winding black ribbon bordered with leaning alder trees.

Barges putt-putt along.

Smells of clinker, coal dust, gasoline.

Boats half sunken in the grey water.

Looking for a man with captain at the front of his name.

Barge which was painted dirty red.

White stripe on its funnel.

Walks the tow path but finds no boat of this description.

Captain sitting on a crate.

Though when he asks at other boats both are known.

Don't suppose you know where he is?

Moves around should be here soon now it's spring.

Anyone taken notice of a boy?

Stayed with him.

Sull young 'n.

Seventeen, eighteen year old.

Quiet like, anyways.

Sit on a hatch for hours without saying a word.

Watch the current.

Stare at the waterflies dancing their sun dance over the ripples.

Leaning over the rails.

Back arched just like a cat.

Beasts and birds are especially his friends.

Bend down to the ground and listen sometimes for hours.

Amongst the riverside grasses.

Watch ants for days.

Know what became of him?

Ever watched ants?

Kind that leave the merest blur behind them.

Spring up out of nothing one fine day and return there.

Best talk to the captain.

Thank 'ee.

Trundled along in a distracted state staring into the canal.

Murky river flowing sluggishly.

Animal carcasses, trash, rotting hulks and tree limbs.

Though as the sun climbs above the trees and its rays penetrate the surface a different water is revealed.

Clear and green with trailing moss braided over the gravel bars.

Rippled with the rises of fish.

Bends for a closer look.

Bream suddenly swam right up to me.

Peered at me with its round bird-like eyes and dived deep down into the water.

Standing again it is as if he sees this place for the first time.

Bushes, nettles and briars entangled along the silent waterway.

Tall bearded grass.

Gazed over the floating houses.

Linked to terra firma by flower-bedecked gangways.

Bird fluttered above its perch on a mossy stone.

Dove that art in the cleft.

Inspected the grass beneath.

Twisting progress of a caterpillar.

Itinerary of a file of ants.

20

Walking along in the spring sunshine he looked down at the road under his feet.

Holes in the asphalt exposed the soil beneath.

Little green leaves were growing.

On his way through the stadtpark the pebbles caught his attention.

Grass spurted between the loose cobblestones.

Among the weeds of the vacant lot concealed in a rusty can.

Geranium burning red.

Sending roots down into the piles of detritus.

So I discovered the sunken door and so I came up for the first time.

See a crack open and a different city appear.

Second, secret city.

Walls full of cracks and festooned with green creeping plants.

Strange bushes whose names no one knows.

Wild flowers.

Growing out of a tiny crevice.

Buses pouring poison but the flowers surviving, garnet roses, pale lilacs.

Potted trees outside restaurants.

Tracks everywhere over the dusty tiles of birds and mice and lizards.

Rats that come out in the hours before dawn.

As long as a man's foot.

Heard the crows in the morning. Their harsh call.

Thrushes at dusk.

The tilt of a guttering and a cat's progress along it.

House cats and stray cats.

Wild sandy ram cat.

Swishes his tail and looks me in the eye.

Started looking at places as if through the round eyes of a cat.

Prowl the outer boulevards.

Peering over fences.

Venturing into more and more cattish places, climbed roofs, straddled railings.

No longer in the law-abiding workaday world.

No visible boundaries between one state or another — no passport examination or customs house.

City of cats and the city of men exist one inside the other.

Between the planks and the barbed wire.

Beyond a half rusted gate.

Narrow passages where human life huddles.

Bulging forms under piled-up cardboard boxes and rags.

Bolthole among sacks of sawdust.

Little rank garden with a small abandoned-looking building at the far end.

Weeds were waist high and you could lie down and hide in them.

Wander the streets in the early hours of the morning rooting around in the rubbish heaps.

Browsed the pavement unceasingly.

Always something to be scavenged.

Packets of crumbling crackers.

Crusts of cheese.

Bottle of milk on the doorstep.

Eyes now digging into the cellars, the foundations, the wells.

Peep out of manholes and drainpipes.

Assume the posture of a cat.

Running with bent back and with hands near the ground, like a beast and yet not of beast shape.

21

Night was like felt.

Cluster of dirt streets.

Lurid drinks and cheap cigarettes.

Shops where tattoos are drawn on sailors' skin.

Artist arranging needles and inks and pierced patterns on his bench.

Ear-piercers, bump-readers.

Old men in their turbans and white shorts.

Bent over cards.

Face in the light of the naphtha flares.

Shabby looking hotel called the Hotel Indio.

Inscription on a large stone in the wall.

Red-painted letters.

Consultations a l'intérieur pour tarot, boules de cristal.

Madame Ruth.

Corridor lit by a greenish glow.

Odours of incense and hot wax.

La bohème.

Heavy coloured stones in her ears and heavy rings on her fingers.

Flowing gypsy dress.

You've come.

Been expecting you.

Voice had a muffled sound as if something was throbbing deep under it.

Eyes were brown, sensitive and shrewd.

Knew he was in pain.

Su mano.

Don't be afraid.

Gave her his hand and she took it and turned it palm up and held it in hers and studied it.

Know what's in your mind.

Monsieur Felix.

Traced his palm with the tip of her finger.

Man with a secret hidden in him.

Put out her arms as if after a retreating figure.

Face of one lost in reverie.

Heard a light sigh.

Ain't gonna see him no more in this world.

Spell was snapt.

Tell me what you want.

Following a will o' the wisp.

Kicked himself loose of the earth.

Vain to follow for I shall learn no more of him nor of his deeds.

Human's not a rabbit or a lynx.

Man couldn't find a trail.

Need a little help.

Eyes sparked greenly in the lamplight.

Things separate from their story have no meaning.

Truth may often be carried about by those who themselves remain all unaware of it.

Shadow knowledge that sometimes comes long before knowledge itself.

Tell me what to do, he said. I'll do anything you say.

Took his hand, drawing him to her side.

Traced the line where it circled under the base of his thumb.

Wander wherever it was needed for as long as it took.

Paths that are seldom trodden.

Footsteps of those who used to cross them.

Should manifest itself.

You mean like I'll get a sign tell me which way to go?

God alone tells futures.

People knew the story of their lives how many would then elect to live them.

Come to know it all in god's good time.

Submit to chance.

Eyes lost in their darkly shadowed hollows.

Hand touching her thigh as though she carried a knife in her garter belt.

22

Late afternoon.

Waters of the canal.

Reddish-coloured barge.

Light was burning in the cabin.

Called captain as he climbed the ladder.

Boatman poked his hairy head out of the window.

Glazed bleary eyes.

Kin come in.

Breakfast with the captain.

Eight in the morning or two in the afternoon meant nothing.

Hadn't had anything to eat since the afternoon of the previous day.

Take a look around the barge.

Had to stoop.

Forgive me, he said, but the ceiling is too low.

Odour of mildew, urine and rotten wood.

Two of the windows had been broken out; they were papered with cardboard and stuffed with rags.

Floor lay a grey-green mould.

Have some grub.

Pot of coffee.

Two dry rolls.

Pray take the basket chair.

Coffee seemed to revive him.

Face was ageing, saggy, full of the disgust of life and the thickening effects of liquor, but it had a hard cheerfulness that I liked and the eyes were as bright as drops of dew.

Twenty years on this boat.

Old life lay behind in the mists.

Boy like a stray dog or cat that attaches itself to you, you don't know quite how it happens.

Found him sleeping under the tarp one rainy morning.

Living like a mouse.

Told me he had been in prison.

No one has the right to pass judgement.

Ever go on your knees and pray for deliverance for all your sins and scoundrel's acts?

Not got any of the mean ways of a bum.

More like a child than a man.

Animal that attempts to make itself as small as possible.

Talked little, ate little.

Get his bearings from signs known only to him.

Crows close their eyes do you know what they see?

121

Birds and beasts do not tell tales.

Though he liked to listen.

Told him about the waters and ways I've travelled.

Trails of men who had gone before.

Interested in roots.

Country you can't dig six feet without uncovering skulls and leg bones.

Men of another time living in the caves.

Pipe had gone out.

Filled it from a pouch, tamped it down and struck a match.

Glowed brightly for a moment.

Go off for a night or two but always came back.

One fine day he disappeared and this time it was for good.

On your own so be it. If that's the way you want it.

Who wants to be fenced in if you don't have to?

Better than being walled in by a house, better than breathing in spoiled air and feeling caged like a varmint.

Shrugged and raised his glass.

Contemplating the water.

So does life swing like a river cuts its banks.

Sat side by side.

Under the moon drinking wine.

Prow of the boat.

Watched the shadows of things emerge.

Journey I have thought of many times.

Gone north in my youth I might have got to be a mountain man.

Lakes and runnin' water and grass to the stirrups.

Voice quavering in the cold.

Night deepened and began to ebb.

Faint glimmering of the coming day in the sky.

Stands to take his leave.

Thanked the old man but the old man did not answer.

23

Night to night the stone city lost its value.

Crosses and recrosses the city until the aimlessness of his walking eventually becomes obvious.

Street seemed absorbed in its own preoccupations.

Building which he passed every day was revealed to him in its reality.

The garbage cans, the stairwells, the door handles, the radiators, the lampshades, the wallpaper.

Four walls of my flat.

Lifted the thin curtain and peered out of the window.

Hazed out-of-focus eyes as though being cooped up in the city and temporarily robbed of their distances had also robbed them of the power of sight.

Time there had outlived itself.

Northland world was calling to him.

Stirring of old instincts which at stated periods drives men out from the sounding cities.

Thing that was not called north but was at the same place.

Spreads out the transcripts on the table.

Oil company road map.

Marking the spot of each sighting or alleged sighting.

Network of meridians and parallels extends from this point across valleys, clearings and marshes.

Patterns that were maps of the world.

Tries again marking only entries that can be corroborated or match the boy in his mind.

Two people saw him as he passed over this ground.

Small ragged figure.

Hollered at him friendly but he went by with his eyes down like he was deef.

Traced the route.

Stared hard at the map.

Not really so much a map as a picture of a voyage.

One long red line.

Es un fantasma, he said.

But isn't that what he is doing?

Chasing ghosts.

Imaginary lines for which there are no reliable benchmarks.

Measured the road with a piece of string and looked at it and measured again.

Drew stick figures on the map.

Unfolds the page with the boy's mugshot.

Held up the paper so that the sunlight shone full upon it.

Examined it for some time.

Put his face together in his mind.

Gradually he detaches himself from the photo, comes to life, and I see him walking down a boulevard under the trees.

Roadside just on the edge of town.

See now what I must do.

Slip into overalls and tennis shoes and clamber over the wall.

Go thy way forth.

Accompanying Felix on his voyage.

Channels out of the city.

Open country.

Following him along the winding riverbank, across sand bars, through groves of cottonwood.

Upward into the mountains.

Pursuer and pursued.

Shadow to shadow in his tracks.

Everything has a shadow of some kind. Maybe even a shadow has a shadow.

24

Days were hot, the evenings flushed.

Seeing out his time in the prison.

Making his rounds from wings to workshops.

Quadrangle to the gateshack.

Numbed to everything about human beings except that they pressed close around you all the time.

Mind had begun to dwell on the north for long stretches.

Something inside me stretched as I walked so that at the same time I was walking on the top of those hills.

Nights he would spend in his room.

Looking out the window, waiting for it to be time to leave.

Cars honked along the alley.

Smell of fuel mix, disinfectants, hot railroad tracks.

Thumbing through an old world atlas, studying the maps.

How steep were these mountains, how wide was this river, how thick were these jungles.

In his imagination the damp walls disappeared and the room was a green farm among the fields.

Had already stopped living there.

Disposed of his remaining belongings.

Cartons to the charity shop on the high street.

Pawn the penitentiary suit.

Manuscripts and other documents gathered into a pile.

Contents into the kitchen stove, lighting the paper with a match.

Reduced to ashes.

Intoxication of cutting all ties.

Slipping away without providing an explanation.

Canvas bag in which a few fundamental things were packed.

Shirt and some underclothing.

Packet of biscuits and a can of sardines.

Notebooks and slips of paper.

Grey army blanket.

Time comes to leave.

Earliest risers were just beginning to look sleepily from their windows.

Street lamps throw out a cold light.

Eased the pack on his shoulders.

Locked the round door.

Lightly on my way.

Through the backstreets and across the railroad tracks.

Bridge over the river.

Walking while the sky paled.

Noise and traffic gradually increased.

Shops began to be unclosed and a few scattered people were met.

Groups of labourers going to their work.

Walked on for a long time passing many large gardens and gentlemen's houses.

Factories of the suburbs.

Outskirts of the town.

City suddenly stopped and you were confronted by open fields.

Elm trees faintly stirring.

Quarter mile down the road he stopped and looked back.

Dark bowl of the town.

Nothing behind me any more.

Gaze now was no longer that of a city dweller.

Existence was no more than what I saw before me.

25

Walked steadily all day.

Sun was well up and felt good on his back.

Air seemed to kiss one's skin.

Turned off the highway at junction.

Drifted under the bridge, past the quiet railway station, the orchards, the meadows.

Passed people now and then.

Walked with his eyes cast slightly downward.

Road winding in and out, now losing itself from my view, and again, further on, reappearing.

Thin ribbon to the horizon.

Plodded on.

Sun swam across the sky.

Hole in the road suddenly wink like a cyclops.

Few miles further.

Lilac evening.

Looking for a place to spend the night.

Came to a stile at the fence.

Old rabbit-bitten pasture with a foot track wandering across it.

Through a thicket of slender oaks.

Narrow plank bridge.

Tiredness on him like a weight.

Turned aside from the path and went into the shadow of the deeper woods.

Settled his shoulders against the base of a tree.

Roughness of the bark.

Ate cold food and settled down on a bed of leaves.

Head resting on my little bundle of clothes.

Blanket over his shoulders.

Darkness lay around me.

Sting of aloneness.

Woke he judged it to be about three.

Lay on his back and looked at a night sky shot with stars.

Near like spiritual bodies.

Hearing and other senses sharpened.

Rustle of the leaves overhead.

Smell of the wet sod.

Day came pale from the east.
Dove called three lonesome, clear, haunting notes.

Couple of squirrels set on a limb and jabbered at me.

Choicest part of a new day is the first of it.

Got up and shook myself.

Biscuit I can eat.

Pursued my journey to the northward.

26

Tramped the edge of the road.

Gravel crunching under the heels of my boots.

Along the hedgerows and borders of coppices.

Back roads of the countryside.

Followed their original tracks, drawn by packhorse or lumbering cartwheel, hugging the curve of a valley.

Cars that came by were farmer cars.

Trucks, tractors.

Ate some berries which I found hanging on the trees.

Slaked my thirst at the brook.

Slept that night in a wash in the river sand with the cane and willow thick about him.

All day the day following through rolling hill country.

Whole morning working round a hill.

Sleeping village.

Buy two hops bread for a cent apiece.

Dime's worth of cheese.

Up the lane through dappled light and shade.

Hum of voices.

Under an olive tree a group of girls.

Chattering stopped and they turned their heads all together.

Offered me an unblinking cluster of eyes.

Lipsticked mouths.

Corner of the road a mile further.

Along the fence line.

Pressed two strands of wire apart and eased himself through.

Strike out across the fields.

Glade circled by slim willows and small cottonwoods.

Sat under the shade of the willows and ate.

Sparrows collect the breadcrumbs.

Leaves that fall from the trees serve him as napkins.

Went on again.

Less used roads.

Path across the fields.

Moving according to my gut feel.

Sense of direction that animals possess perfectly also awakes in man under the right conditions.

Hares ran across his path.

Farmer driving hogs down a lane.

Sleeping on piles of fresh bracken.

Hole in a haystack.

Wherever dark fell on ye.

Nights were fine and sleeping out of doors was a pleasure.

Watching the fireflies sparkle.

Dry croaking of frogs.

Trembling sometimes with the thrill of being free.

Once I awoke with an animal sleeping on my legs.

A cat or a rat or a rabbit.

Quick dark shape.

Lay awake till dawn.

Listening to the small noises.

Grasshoppers chawing.

Night speech of plant and stone.

Awoke with a start in broad daylight to see a man standing in front of him.

Farmer with a shotgun.

Get off my land before I put the dog on you.

Dog steaming from the mouth.

Next time this young varmint sets foot on my land you can eat him.

Took my bundle in my hand.

Skirted villages.

Making wide circles around farmhouses.

Sleeping in thickets, in oases of rushes, under tall reeds.

Hollow out of the wind.

Following the contours of the land.

Courses of the rivers.

Ever followed in his track.

Yonder to the north.

Walked on as though keeping a vow.

27

Day by day he changed.

Walk lighter, stumble less.

Grew callous to all ordinary pain.

Lost the fastidiousness which had characterised his old life.

Washing potatoes for breakfast in a pond.

Ate a turnip like an apple.

Few acorns to assuage the pangs of hunger.

Little food is required to sustain a life on the edge.

Satisfied just by earth and water and trees and the sky over him.

Tracks worn through the forest and over the hills.

Once, in the heat of the day, he stripped off his clothes and submerged himself in the water of a lonely dam.

Wash my socks.

Bake dry upon the stones.

Looks at his feet in the sun, rubs his blisters and takes the dirt from between his toes.

Bathed by feelings.

Even the weeds moved him.

Seemed somehow removed from the passage of time.

Land taking you back to something that was familiar, something you had known at some time but forgotten.

Rest against a piece of granite.

Quiet under the long shadows of early evening.

Morning he presses on.

Avoiding inhabited places.

Walking ever deeper into the woodland.

Encountered few people.

Solitary horseman.

Campfires of gypsies squatting by little streams.

Shades of twilight were beginning to settle upon the earth.

Day tending to its end.

Loping stride.

Bounded right onto the ashes of a campfire that was still smoking.

Old man small and bent.

More frightened than I was.

Tried awkwardly to run off or to hide.

I don't have anything, he said. You can look if you want.

Dressed in rags.

Each of his boots was of different colour.

Round the waist of his mackintosh, which was belted with string, hung a collection of pots and spoons.

145

Gathered some dry sticks.

Soon had a fire.

Billy of tea in the red flames.

Face in the small light streaked with black.

Oakmoss bearded.

Eye was overgrown by a cataract and he kept his head tilted as if he were trying to see around it.

Spoke in whispers.

Walkin' this country for years.

Always on the road. You can't stay in one place.

Nowhere to go but everywhere.

The oveja negra, no?

Scratched the back of his neck.

Began pulling off his boots.

Unwound the rags.

Horny foot.

Perfume of musk and piss.

Nice fire to warm your shins.

Start to cough.

Shaking up like a old engine.

Things he has seen.

Crossing and recrossing the country every year, south in the winter and north in the summer.

North to the mountains.

Once found, the path was easy to follow.

Drew me a map in the mud.

In the gloomy dirt with his broken fingernail saying north were that direction.

Rattling some cough from deep down.

Voice when he spoke again sounded sober and quiet and tired to death.

You need to go on, he said. I can't go with you.

Queer gleam in his eye.

Haggard and hollow.

Waits for the soft dry throat rattle that will free him.

28

North along the river track.

Narrow paths among the folded lands.

Backwoods routes.

Deeper into the forest.

Untilled land.

Followed the tracks of wild creatures.

Wildcats and foxes.

Nibbled at roots and bulbs.

Cut my wants down to the bare bones.

After a few days without food one's hunger becomes dulled.

New leanness and knowledge and wisdom.

JEREMY GAVRON

Learned to listen to the birds.

Sounds of earth and trees.

Remove my shoes.

Walk barefoot in the grass.

Bark of fallen trees.

Feet grew hard to the trail.

Knowledge comes from my soles.

Best not to walk on the track but to keep a few hundred metres away.

Take advantage of every cover.

Colour of the place you're in.

Picked up a handful of dirt.

Rubbed the dirt into my shoes and clothes, into the skin of my hands and face.

Blend into the surroundings and become invisible.

Like a mossy stalk.

150

A rock among rocks.

Pass unseen and unheard.

Buried his faeces.

Remnants of food.

Morning came I would set out again on my journey, leaving nothing to tell.

Like fish through water or birds through air.

Road that had to be crossed, and especially every bridge, represented a danger.

Crouched above the road beneath the fir trees.

Edges of the forest you can see without being seen.

Trucks are humming past.

Lines of cars.

Crept in and out of the clefts of the rocks.

Down the bank.

Ran across the road.

Ducked into the shelter of the woods.

Deepest forest was the greatest security.

Cloven track between tall trees.

Paths overgrown with brambles.

Haunting the thickets.

Lingering morning.

Winding through the undergrowth.

Rain falling amid the foliage.

Found himself in front of houses. Ruins.

Village that has been abandoned by all its inhabitants.

Little houses of stone nestling close to one another, perched on top of each other.

Flat-topped cedars growing out of the cracks.

Walked through the ghost village.

Pieces of decaying machinery, a stack of rusty nails.

Inside the little rooms water jars and bowls.

A book. It had lost its covers.

Thumbed through the heavy bloated pages.

Spotted and stained.

Got ahead of books.

Made his way out into the cold grey light.

Remains of a small temple.

Roof had collapsed and only a few feet of the side walls still stood.

Weeds, grass and shrubs growing wild.

Burial ground no longer used.

Wooden crosses sticking up here and there.

Gravestones leant together.

Skeletons lying on their backs in the dirt down below.

29

Countryside was changed, the summer past.

Leaves turned red. The purple blooms of thistles became black.

Days grow shorter.

Had been on the trail six weeks.

Seven weeks.

Lost track of the day.

Thought the month was October but he wasn't sure.

Come a good peace and have been lucky with the weather.

Morning mists were rising.

Growing colder.

Sleep with my feet in the bag.

Hands between his thighs.

Clothes much consumed by the country.

Shoes were pretty ragged by now.

Hole that have a little socks in them.

Plodding along.

Grimy and hungry eyed.

Tired down into his bones.

North because it had become a habit.

Sometimes, as he walked, he did not know whether he was awake or asleep.

Mind had broken the leash, spurred on by fatigue.

Memory rising as if it has been pursuing me.

Cobwebby dreams of my past life.

Out of the tired cloud of his mind Ma's face appeared, the dark and watery eyes.

Stooping figure.

Father who had never been comfortable with people.

Remembered all — every pinochle game, every woman, every sad night.

Thoughts congealing.

Human being survives by his ability to forget.

Feels a tug at his heels from hands growing up through the grass.

Dreamed that I saw my mother and it seemed as though she saw me but then turned her back on me.

Weather had turned bad.

Rained often, sometimes in sudden downpours.

Walk beneath the dripping trees.

Garments all were dank.

Feet mechanical.

Stumbling over roots and stones.

Fell headlong.

So weary that for some time he did nothing save rest upon the ground.

Face on the pillow of brown moist earth.

Began to shake with cold.

Felt of his right leg.

Ankle had begun to swell painfully.

Gash just above his knee.

Got up on his feet and essayed to walk.

Covered with mud, lame, half-blind.

Trail losing itself in the dark and the trees hunched close around.

Saw a hole and crept up it.

Hollow of a giant horse-chestnut tree.

Crouched inside and spent the night huddled there.

Daylight came slow and gloomy.

Hobbled forward.

Using a branch as a walking stick.

Drinking from rivulets.

Beard dipped into the water.

Ate handfuls of flowers and his stomach hurt.

Emerged upon the slope of a down.

Path across the fields.

Norther had blown in about mid morning.

See the rain coming across the country in a grey wall.

Nothing you could do except put one foot forward and then the other.

Bent over against the cold.

Wet to the skin.

Dusk turned to night.

Path down a densely wooded gully.

Pulled himself into some thick bushes and lay flat with his head on his arm.

Back against the cold earth.

Leg was throbbing.

Tried to lick some water from the uneven ground.

Sucked at his soaked trousers.

Awakened sick and trembling with cold in the first flush of the morning.

So weak that he could scarcely raise himself into a sitting position.

Limbs were almost powerless.

Stiff clear to his bones.

Had to get out of that gully and that part of the wild country soon or he was a gone goose.

Crept along on his elbows and one good knee.

Like any four-legged creature.

Leg dragging.

Felt his strength leaving him.

Every breath he took was like a razor.

Trees and rocks about him seemed shadowy and dim.

No longer feel his hands.

Had escaped too completely from men. Nature would kill him now.

Long to let go, drift free of things.

Last stubbornness to live.

Ridge about forty foot high.

Shivering and sweating and soaked with rain he came up over the edge.

Little farmhouse stood near a creek.

Half hidden in the trees.

Crawl toward it.

Through the bushes, down the knoll.

House was dark.

Called cooee but it were long abandoned.

Raised the latch. The door yielded to the pressure.

30

Cobwebs stringy with dirt.

Rude table — a plank on two posts; a heap of rubbish reposed in a dark corner.

Narrow iron bedstead.

Lay down on the bed with my coat.

Tattered blanket.

Taste of fever in his mouth.

Slept unquiet.

Saw faces, heard voices.

Thought the country was saying something to him.

Wind was trying to whisper something to me and I couldn't

make out what it was.

Something else like the faint fall of soft bare feet.

Looked up to see a little boy.

Face amongst the leaves on the level with my own looking at me very fierce and steady.

Sense he wanted to tell me something.

Woke with a sudden start.

Violent pains in my head and feaverish.

Not strength to stand up or to get myself any water to drink.

Realised that the footsteps were nothing but the sound of my own heart.

Evening he was delirious again.

Night was moving now. He tried not to look at it, but it was true — the night moved in waves, fluttering.

Idea his body wasn't his.

Observer of this man who lies here.

Woke up in a sweat.

Aching and trembling in every limb.

In and out of lucidity.

Unaccountably I think about a girl I talked to once.

Touched me on my left shoulder.

Attic room.

Hips were so narrow.

Perching at the sleeper's bedside.

Don't live nowheres no more, she said.

Little hand on my shoulder as she spoke those words.

Thought that she was crying.

Woke in the cold dark, coughing.

Wind had dropped, not a leaf stirred; and the silence was total, broken only at intervals by a rustle of wings or the sad cry of some distant nocturnal bird.

Stalks of light poked through.

Thirst. Great thirst.

Felt of his leg carefully, finger tips probing.

Swollen almost twice its size.

Got up on his good leg and slowly shifted his weight.

Bad leg hurt but it bore up.

Pulled the door open.

Little stream.

Bent over like a squirrel.

Drank from it with the hollow of his hand.

Water was the only medicine he had and he put faith in it.

Face toward the house again.

Good strong sleep.

Living life returned.

Swaying on my gimpy leg.

Opened a few windows and shutters.

Debris of leaves and pine needles, webs, cocoons and insect corpses.

Foul smell drifted from his body.

Went back to the stream.

Wading out into the middle of it, bad leg and all, and gulped water and splashed his face.

Washed his hands and beard.

Sand for soap.

Soaked his calluses.

Stream were like a poultice.

Awoke stronger from each short slumber.

Lying under the open window with the sun in his face.

Tried to guess the date, counting in silence, or rather groping over nights and days. His beard informed him better than his brain.

Time for me to leave.

Checked his bum leg.

Swelling was going down.

Face in a grey webby window.

Gaunt, brown.

Eyes half buried.

Shirt hung in tatters.

Shoes have a big hole like they laughing.

Opened the door and went out.

Down to the brook and began to climb along its course.

31

Cows raised their muzzles out of the grass and regarded him.

Cars that passed gave him all the berth.

Man at the petrol station.

Wonder if you could tell me what day this is.

Gave me such an unreal look.

Bought milk.

Drinking it as I sat on a railing of the bridge.

Frail hopeful lunatic tipping the carton to quiet his stomach.

Road into town.

People passing in the street turned to look at him.

Rest on a bench in front of the church.

Drunk on milk.

Before entering an inn I hesitate outside.

Who is this that cometh out of the wilderness?

Innkeeper with his green apron.

Ask about spending the night and he studies me first from head to toe.

Twelve marks including breakfast.

Come into the parlour, sir.

Old low-roofed room with a great beam across the middle of the ceiling and benches with high backs to them.

Gave me some lemonade.

Dark bread, plentiful cheese and butter.

Coffee service with cups and cream pitcher and a sugar bowl.

Conducted to his chamber.

Hot bath.

Up to the elbows with red patches and sores.

So thin his teeth hurt.

Lay down and a dead sleep closed on him.

Sun was up so high when I waked.

Grateful for a day of rest.

Hearty meal.

Baskets of hot loaves, great yellow blocks of butter, strings of sausages, mountains of potatoes.

Ate until he couldn't any more.

Slept more.

Stars were coming out when I woke.

Nothing about but the wind and the silence.

Empty mind of sleep.

Day to day.

Recovering his strength.

Bought socks and underwear.

Hickory shirt.

Pair of understandin's.

Treading it slowly.

Edge of the town.

Crossed the river just above the pool by some stepping stones.

On up the hillside.

Every day I tried another path.

Across the hillocks and vales.

Up fells and screes.

Down into the oaks.

Sometimes a shepherd's hut or a distant man walking.

Grey roofs of the farmsteadings.

Most of the time I was alone.

Air was thick.

Stones crack in the frosty night.

On the pond swims a membrane of ice.

Whispering snow.

Fell all night and the next day.

Nothing to do but sleep.

Glass of mild and bitter and sit down by a table near the fire.

Smoke if you had anything to smoke and think if you had anything to think about.

Sky slowly grew lighter.

Broke new.

Walked up the hill.

Snow which had not yet felt the foot of man.

Looks out over the snowy rooftops of the town to the snowy moor.

White and grey of the mountains.

Them rocks somewhere.

Body had been found.

Shepherd cried out in amazement.

Way from his cabin to the sheepfold.

Crook in his hand.

Final step.

Visit the scene.

Confront the shepherd.

32

Sunset the trail arrives at the hill village.

Low public house.

Tap room in the rear of the premises.

Several rough men in smock frocks, drinking and smoking.

Looked at him as if he were something rare.

Sat down in the farthest corner.

Ordered some dinner.

Pieces of meat.

Loaf of coarse bread.

Conversation of the men assembled here turned upon the neighbouring land and farmers.

Tired with the walk, and getting up so early, he dozed a little.

Had almost dropped asleep when he was half wakened by the noisy entrance of a newcomer.

Signal for various homely jokes with the countrymen.

Eyed him from time to time.

Finally the man asked.

Who are you sir and why exactly are you here?

Here on a mission.

Secrets of the mountains in search of something still unknown.

Fate of Felix.

How and why the kid died.

Many months this has been my task.

Man nodded.

Smoking a cigarette and he raised it to his lips.

Spoke in a high clear voice.

All these writers snooping around to find out what they can.

Aiming to conconct a story.

Books what turning out to be best sellers.

How are people to know that it's all lies.

Something grown out of the snow.

Pale skin of words.

Man could tell his true history.

Was not words.

Finished his cigarette and let fall the stub of it.

Hands folded one across the other before him as if there were no more to be said.

First flush of the morning.

Village road.

Sheep pen at the foot of the hills.

Man came out and leaned on a manure fork.

Winter in his grey eyes.

What can I do for you?

Understand you found the body.

Thought you could give me some details.

Nodded at me gravely.

Spoke with great circumspection and courtesy.

Life was spent among bleak mountains.

Looking after lost sheep.

Nature of his profession that his experience with death should be greater than for most.

All his years.

Never to this day seen a stout manchild laid out.

Save one.

Cold and stiff.

Buried in drifts of snow.

No wound or bruise upon his person to show how he had met his dreadful end.

No more'n a scratch.

Covered the boy with his slicker.

Wouldn't become carrion for the birds of prey.

Eyes picked out by the crows.

Walked down.

Call the police.

Carried his small body off to the morgue.

Frail burden of bones and skin.

Gaze ride high.

Northward slope of the hill.

Shading his eyes with his hand.

Ask you a few questions.

Told you know the mountains as well as any man.

What happened in the middle of that stormy night?

How did he pass the last moments of his life?

What is your theory?

What you think?

Tell the police.

Come beyond the limits of his world.

No man could cross those mountains in the darkness.

Teeth of a snowstorm.

Come a long way.

To this place today to find you.

Wish to hear your real, real opinion.

To understand.

Moment's pause of hesitation.

Head came up slowly.

Tell you a story they used to tell around here.

Quick dark shape that hid behind the rocks.

Small hunched figure.

Steal bread under the cover of darkness.

Running monkey-like, bent double, over fences and through bushes.

Mud flying from his feet.

You see him?

Once he saw a wolf loping along a ridge.

Something that wasn't there.

Looked toward him with her yellow eyes.

Where he come from?

Go to sleep?

Lifting his hand he pointed.

Bandits' lairs, untrodden spots.

Cave or a crack which could never be suspected from below.

181

Only when some nanny goat wandered or got stranded here might a shepherd risk his life to climb up.

Summer the cave was better than a house.

Have a stream and it cool.

Live like an animal.

Voice slowed down.

Look an old man gets when he's telling a story he's thought about but never told before.

Something very strange.

Didn't tell the coppers.

No one would believe.

Studying the tracks for some sign.

Marks of his footsteps in the snow.

Barefoot human prints.

Prints of a second animal.

Hooves of sheep.

Strange wild story seemed to have come to us from amid the mad elements.

Wild snow fall.

So thick a man couldn't be seen two paces away.

Wandering lost.

Shivering in every limb.

Grazing my knees, hitting my shoulder against a stone wall.

Sheep that had strayed.

Approached me in the semi-darkness bleating at me.

Come up and nosed me.

Cuddling against me as if I could offer a solution.

Provided me with a warmth.

Reek of udder balm.

Immersion in pure sheepness.

Fell asleep alongside.

Hummock where I lie.

Daggy sheep.

Some time during the night it had drifted off.

Saw where the snow had been pawed away.

Eyes from one print to the next.

Quarter mile straight to a rock outcrop.

Makest thy flock.

Left Felix to his fate.

Go to the land of souls.

33

Sunshine like a day in spring.

Brown bracken sticks to the ground.

Patches of snow.

Followed a narrow, sinuous track cut into the hill.

Shepherd had come the same way.

Climbing steadily.

Narrow path worn deep into the stone ledges.

Sheep paths.

Trudge and pant and climb and slip and climb and gasp.

Came to an outcrop of rock.

Inquired of the shepherd.

Hollow in which the body had been found.

Not find a more lonely tract.

High moor where the wind hissed through the heather.

Queer small crows of the high places.

Skeleton of a sheep.

Stood for a while.

Silver breaths.

Sore and heavy laden.

Bird screech.

Overhead the great lammergeier turns and turns.

Old buzzard knows something.

All tales are one.

All worldly pursuits have but one unavoidable and inevitable end.

Well, kid, I thought, you can have yourself a long rest now.

Resumed his trudge.

Climb took energy from his thoughts and sent it to his legs and hips.

Weariness came over the face of the sun.

Brows of the broken cliffs.

Peculiar formation in the rocks; two rounded ledges, one directly over the other, with a mouth-like opening between.

Crawl up.

Clambering over ice.

Orifice into the throat of the cave.

Smelled stale and damp.

Boot kicked something that clattered on the stones.

Had been a fire there.

Floor was smooth and the walls and roof would protect him from the night's wet chill.

Drew together a mess of fire leavings.

Charred stubs.

Log ends not consumed.

Started a blaze.

Breath of the cavern carried the smoke outside.

Roof of the cave was red and brown.

Sat leaning forward studying the flames.

Peace among these looming rocks.

Thought that maybe he could live the rest of his life like this.

Cave of his own ken.

Peed near the entrance to let animals know.

Bed on the rocks.

Curled up asleep like a bear.

Heart of the earth silence.

Unexpectedly I find myself near tears.

Hope died within Felix.

Stepped over the edge while I had been permitted to draw back my hesitating foot.

Sign that I must entrust myself to life.

Stories did not begin at the beginning or conclude with a happy ending, but they flickered in the half light, wound round themselves, emerged from the mists for a moment.

Like these rocks and sky and snow.

Tree will not deny its roots.

What man be free from the air him breathe or set a-loose from the ground what's under his two feets?

Must cease his wanderings and make for himself some place in the world.

Fit himself back among people.

Huddled close to the small fire.

Drifted off into grey sleep.

Awoke not long after dawn.

Circle of daylight.

Buried the embers of the fire.

Saw something.

Behind the corner of stone.

Bent down.

Jacket threadbare.

Old curled up boots.

Sat in the hollow of the rock.

Felt the wrinkled, slightly moist touch of cloth.

Smell of thy garments.

Tells all and it tells nothing.

Said that god offers man the choice between repose and truth.

Storyteller's task.

Live in the midst of the incomprehensible.

Set the cloth on the ground.

Broken boots.

Crawled out through the stone lips.

Sun came up upon the left.

Picked a path.

Sliding and tumbling.

Down the mountain in long bounds.

Reaching the road.

Set loose once more into the world to see what I would make of it.

End is not yet told.

AUTHOR'S NOTE

The great majority of the lines ... are extracted word for word from the hundred and ... by the thirty-nine authors listed below. Fourteen ... the ... last nine, are made up entirely of ... lines.

Appelfeld, Aharon. *The Story of a Life* ...

Appelfeld, Aharon. *Tzili, it Dayichla*

Ballard, J.G. *The Drowned World*

Barker, Pat. *Regeneration*.

Bellow, Saul. *Herzog*.

Bolaño, Roberto. *Distant Star* ...

Böll, Heinrich. *The Lost Honour of Katharina Blum* ... Vanuwitz.

Calvino, Italo. *Invisible Cities*, tr. William Weaver.

Calvino, Italo. *Marcovaldo*, tr. William Weaver.

Calvino, Italo. *The Path to the Spiders' Nests* ... Colquhoun.

Carey, Peter. *True History of the Kelly Gang*.

Cather, Willa. *Death Comes for the Archbishop*.

Cather, Willa. *The Professor's House*.

Chandler, Raymond. *Farewell, My Lovely*.

AUTHOR'S NOTE

The great majority of the lines in this novel are sourced word for word from the hundred or so books, by some eighty authors, listed below. Fourteen of the chapters, including the last nine, are made up entirely of sourced lines.

Appelfeld, Aharon. *The Story of a Life*, tr Aloma Halter.

Appelfeld, Aharon. *Tzili*, tr Dalya Bilu.

Ballard, JG. *The Drowned World*.

Barker, Pat. *Regeneration*.

Bellow, Saul. *Herzog*.

Bolaño, Roberto. *Distant Star*, tr Chris Andrews.

Böll, Heinrich. *The Lost Honour of Katharina Blum*, tr Leila Vennewitz.

Calvino, Italo. *Invisible Cities*, tr William Weaver.

Calvino, Italo. *Marcovaldo*, tr William Weaver.

Calvino, Italo. *The Path to the Spiders' Nests*, tr Archibald Colquhoun.

Carey, Peter. *True History of the Kelly Gang*.

Cather, Willa. *Death Comes for the Archbishop*.

Cather, Willa. *The Professor's House*.

Chandler, Raymond. *Farewell, My Lovely*.

Chandler, Raymond. *The Big Sleep.*

Chandler, Raymond. *The Lady in the Lake.*

Chandler, Raymond. *The Long Good-Bye.*

Clébert, John-Paul. *Paris Vagabond*, tr Donald Nicholson-Smith.

Coetzee, JM. *The Life and Times of Michael K.*

Conan Doyle, Arthur. *The Adventures and The Memoirs of Sherlock Holmes.*

Conan Doyle, Arthur. *The Return of Sherlock Holmes.*

Conrad, Joseph. *Heart of Darkness.*

Coleridge, Samuel Taylor. *The Rime of the Ancient Mariner.*

Defoe, Daniel. *Robinson Crusoe.*

Dick, Philip K. *Do Androids Dream of Electric Sheep?*

Dickens, Charles. *Oliver Twist.*

Dickey, James. *To the White Sea.*

Fitzgerald, F Scott. *The Great Gatsby.*

Gardner, John. *Grendel.*

Genet, Jean. *The Thief's Journal*, tr Bernard Frechtman.

Giono, Jean. *Second Harvest*, tr Henri Fluchère and Geoffrey Myers.

Gordimer, Nadine. *July's People.*

Gorky, Maxim. *My Apprenticeship*, tr Ronald Wilks.

Grass, Günter. *Cat and Mouse*, tr Ralph Manheim.

Greene, Graham. *A Burnt-Out Case.*

Greene, Graham. *The Power and the Glory.*

Grey, Zane. *Riders of the Purple Sage.*

Grossman, David. *Someone to Run With*, tr Vered Almog and Maya Gurantz.

Guthrie, AB. *The Big Sky.*

Haffner, Ernst. *Blood Brothers*, tr Michael Hoffman.

Heaney, Seamus. *Beowulf*.

Herzog, Werner. *Of Walking in Ice*, tr Martje Herzog and Alan Greenberg.

Hesse, Herman. *Steppenwolf*, tr David Horrocks.

Jefferies, Richard. *After London*.

Johnson, Denis. *Train Dreams*.

Kapuściński, Ryszard. *Another Day of Life*, tr William R Brand and Katarzyna Mroczkowska-Brand.

Kee, Robert. *A Crowd is not Company*.

Kelman, James. *How Late it Was, How Late*.

Kerouac, Jack. *On the Road*.

King James Bible.

Koch, Christopher K. *The Year of Living Dangerously*.

Lee, Laurie. *As I Walked Out One Midsummer Morning*.

Levi, Primo. *If Not Now, When?* tr William Weaver.

Lind, Jakov. *Soul of Wood*, tr Ralph Mannheim.

London, Jack. *The Call of the Wild, White Fang, and Other Stories*.

MacGill, Patrick. *Children of the Dead End*.

Manfred, Frederick. *Lord Grizzly*.

Manning, Maurice. *The Common Man*.

Matthiessen, Peter. *The Snow Leopard*.

McCarthy, Cormac. *All the Pretty Horses*.

McCarthy, Cormac. *Cities of the Plain*.

McCarthy, Cormac. *Outer Dark*.

McCarthy, Cormac. *The Crossing*.

McCarthy, Cormac. *The Road*.

McMurtry, Larry. *Lonesome Dove*.

Mitchell, Joseph. *Joe Gould's Secret*.

Mitchell, Joseph. *Up in the Old Hotel*.

Modiano, Patrick. *Missing Person*, tr Daniel Weissbort, Verba Mundi.

Modiano, Patrick. *The Search Warrant*, tr Joanna Kilmartin.

Modiano, Patrick. *Suspended Sentences*, tr Mark Polizzotti.

Mosley, Walter. *A Little Yellow Dog*.

Mosley, Walter. *Devil in a Blue Dress*.

Nabokov, Vladimir. *The Eye*.

Naipaul, VS. *A Bend in the River*.

Naipaul, VS. *Miguel Street*.

Neider, Charles. *The Authentic Death of Hendry Jones*.

Ōe, Kenzaburō. *Death by Water*, tr Deborah Boliver Boehm.

O'Brien, Tim. *Going after Cacciato*.

Orwell, George. *Down and Out in Paris and London*.

Orwell, George. *Nineteen Eighty-Four*.

Oz, Amos. *Panther in the Basement*, tr Nicholas de Lange.

Oz, Amos. *A Tale of Love and Darkness*, tr Nicholas de Lange.

Papadiamantis, Alexandros. *The Murderess*, tr Peter Levi.

Paton, Alan. *Cry, The Beloved Country*.

Schaeffer, Jack. *Shane*.

Schneider, Peter. *The Wall Jumper*, tr Leigh Hafrey.

Schwartz, Delmore. *What Is To Be Given*.

Shalamov, Varlam. *Kolyma Tales*, tr John Glad.

Sciascia, Leonardo. *The Day of the Owl*, tr Archibald Colquhoun and Arthur Oliver.

Selvon, Samuel. *The Lonely Londoners*.

Shelley, Mary. *Frankenstein*.

Simic, Charles. *Dime-Store Alchemy*.

Stevenson, Robert Louis. *The Strange Case of Dr Jekyll and Mr Hyde: and other tales of terror*.

FELIX CULPA

Tolkien, JRR. *The Fellowship of the Ring.*
Twain, Mark. *The Adventures of Huckleberry Finn.*
Williamson, Henry. *Tarka the Otter.*
Woodrell, Daniel. *Winter's Bone.*
Woodrell, Daniel. *Woe to Live On.*
Yoshimura, Akira. *One Man's Justice,* tr Mark Ealey.

197

ACKNOWLEDGEMENTS

My grateful thanks to the MacDowell Colony, where the earliest version of this story was written. And to my colleagues and students in the MFA Program for Writers at Warren Wilson College, whose inspirational teaching and conversation helped to shape this book.

DISCARD